The Jaws of Death

by

Malachy Doyle

Illustrated by Nana Li

To find out more about Malachy Doyle and his books, please visit:
www.malachydoyle.com

First published in 2011 in Great Britain by
Barrington Stoke Ltd
18 Walker St, Edinburgh, EH3 7LP

www.barringtonstoke.co.uk

ISBN: 978-1-84299-402-3

Printed in Great Britain by Bell & Bain Ltd

Contents

Chapter 1
The Fight

Shun-Che, the great master, lifted his arm to attack. The look on his face and the power in his body would put fear into the heart of any man. But not Kwang-Su. Oh, no.

Quicker than lightning, and with no more effort than was needed, Shun-Che's brave young student took one step back, raised his leg high and kicked his master's arm away.

"Uh!" moaned Shun-Che. "You learn well, Kwang-Su. But try this!"

And before the boy could get his balance back, his master grabbed him by the foot, threw him in the air, and Kwang-Su hit the floor with a painful thud.

"Had enough?" The older man stood over him, with a smile. But Kwang-Su wasn't ready to admit defeat. Jumping to his feet, he aimed a blow with his fist at his master's chest.

Shun-Che, surprised by his young student's speed, was too late to stop it. The blow sent him reeling to the ground, and the boy stood above him, in victory.

"Well done, Kwang-Su," gasped his master, as the winner helped him to his feet. "For three years, I have taught you all there is to know. It is time for you to return to your parents and look after them in their old age."

"I shall be sorry to leave you, Master," replied the boy, bowing his head to Shun-Che, "for you have been a great teacher."

"Take my wooden staff with you," Shun-Che said, "for you will make good use of it. And remember, boy – the journey of a thousand miles begins with a single step."

"I will start early," Kwang-Su told him, "and go by the Bridge of Gold."

"No," said his master. "You must go by the Bridge of Indigo, for there you shall meet the woman you will marry."

"But, Master!" Kwang-Su was shocked. "A wife is the last thing I want! I mean to use all the skills you have taught me to become a great hero."

"You are already the bravest of men," replied Shun-Che, "and you will prove it sooner than you think. But that does not mean you should not look after your parents in their old age. And take a wife, also, when you find one who is right for you."

Chapter 2
The Journey Begins

Kwang-Su woke early the next morning and off he went.

Soon he grew thirsty, for it was the hottest of days, so he stopped at a little house by the Bridge of Indigo. There, he asked an old woman for a drink.

The woman called through to her daughter to fetch some water. And as soon as the girl came out, Kwang-Su understood what

Shun-Che, his great master, had told him. For there was something about this young woman that made him feel happier than he had ever felt before.

The old woman was not pleased, though, for she could see how Kwang-Su and her daughter, Ling-Ling, were looking at each other.

"Turn your eyes away, boy!" she hissed. "If I had two girls, you might have had one of them and be welcome, but we are a poor family and Ling-Ling must marry into money. A mandarin, a rich and powerful man from the city, wants to make her his wife."

"But I've told you before, Mother," cried the girl, "I do not want to marry that ugly old man! He must be eighty years old and he has a face like a monkey!"

"You will do as I say, child," replied her mother, crossly. "And as for you ..." she said, turning to Kwang-Su. And then her voice changed from anger to sweetness, for she had come up with a plan – a plan that could make use of Kwang-Su's feelings for her daughter. "Come into the house, boy ..." she said. "There's something I want to show you."

Kwang-Su went in and was surprised by the strong smell of herbs. On a chair in the middle of the room lay a pestle and mortar, made from stone.

"I have used this pestle and mortar to crush and mix herbs for magic potions. I was taught how to make them by powerful Genii," the old woman told him. "Then I sell them to people who are ill, to make them better. That is how my daughter and I have been able to keep going since my husband died. But now that the pestle and mortar are broken, I cannot."

"I will buy you a new pestle and mortar," Kwang-Su offered. For even though the girl's mother had refused to allow him to marry her, he wanted to do all he could to help them both. And maybe, just maybe, the old woman might change her mind.

"Thank you, young man," she replied. "I can see that you are kind at heart, but that would not do at all."

"Why?" asked the boy.

"The pestle and mortar have to be made from a dark green stone called jade. And the only way to replace them is to go all the way to the Genii's home, on a mountain above the Sea of Jewels. If you will do that, Kwang-Su, and bring me back a jade pestle and mortar, my daughter and I will be able to live well enough, without her marrying a rich old mandarin."

"I will do as you ask," said the boy.

Kwang-Su had no idea where the Genii lived, but Ling-Ling took him out into the garden and showed him a line of mountains, far away in the distance, with one snow-capped peak high above the rest.

"That high peak is Mount Fumi," she told him. "The Genii sit in the snow on the top, looking down on the Sea of Jewels. It is a very special place, of many, untold riches. But it is a terrifying place too, for no human has ever been there and come back to tell the tale."

"I am afraid of nothing," said the boy. "For I have studied for three years with the great master, Shun-Che, and he has taught me how to control my fear. Just tell me how to get there."

"First you must cross the Blue River," said the girl, her face lined with worry. "Then the White River, the Red River and the Black River."

"That will be easy, then," said Kwang-Su, "for I am a very good swimmer."

"I'm afraid it won't," Ling-Ling warned him. "Each river is full of enormous fish, who would eat you as soon as you entered the water. That is why my mother has given you this task. In truth, she thinks you will never come back alive, and that if you are dead, I will have no choice but to marry the old, ugly mandarin."

"I'm not afraid of fish!" cried Kwang-Su.

"Maybe not," said the girl. "But I think you should take this with you." And she handed him a small wooden box. "In it are five little red seeds. Throw one in each river as you pass, and it will shrink to a tiny stream, over which you can jump."

Hmmm, thought the boy. *Four rivers but five seeds, I wonder why that is.*

"Promise me one thing …" said Ling-Ling.

"What is that?"

"That you won't try to swim any of the rivers without using them."

Kwang-Su looked at the seeds, each the size of a pea. He did not understand how they could help him but did not wish to be rude to her, so he agreed to do as she said.

"And hurry back!" said Ling-Ling, with a shy little smile. "You don't have much time, if you are to save me from the ugly old mandarin!"

On his way the boy passed through the town of Yo-Chan, where his parents lived. He told them all that had happened since he left home.

"I don't think the Genii will be very happy to see you turning their mighty rivers into streams," his mother warned him, for she was a wise woman, as mothers always are. "If you want them to let you have one of their green jade pestle and mortars, I think you'd better take these with you."

She handed him a second tiny box, and this one held another five little seeds, white this time rather than red.

"Throw one into each stream after you've crossed back over on your way home, and it will become a river again," she told him.

Chapter 3
The Fearful Rivers

In the morning Kwang-Su kissed his father and mother and went on his way.

He rested in the hottest part of the day, carried on when it grew cool, and at the end of seven days he came to the Blue River. It was a quarter of a mile wide, as blue as a summer sky, and the most terrifying fish were pushing their heads up out of the water. Each one was twice the size of a football, and each had the sharpest teeth Kwang-Su had ever seen.

"Help!" muttered the boy, under his breath. "Maybe I'm not as brave as I thought!"

But he had faith in the skills that his master had taught him, and he wanted to believe in Ling-Ling and the power of her little red seeds.

"I might as well see if they work," he said, opening the box. And he pulled one out and tossed it into the water. Straight away, the wide blue river became a little stream and the man-eating fish were no bigger than tadpoles.

Kwang-Su could hardly believe his eyes but, when he'd made sure that it really was safe, he pulled off a shoe and hopped across.

Not long after, he came to the White River. It was half a mile wide, the water foamed and bubbled as it rushed past, and everywhere, under the water and over, were the most enormous, fat sea snakes.

"I won't be able to hop over this one," said Kwang-Su, feeling his courage slipping away from him once more. But he closed his eyes and saw his mother and father.

"Be brave and be strong and believe in the seeds, boy!" they were saying. So he pulled out the second red one and threw it into the water. And to his great delight, the rushing river again shrank to a trickle, and the mighty sea snakes became nothing more than the smallest of eels.

Leaping across, the young man carried on until he reached the Red River. This one took his breath away completely, for it was three-quarters of a mile wide, looked like a great sea of blood, and a row of angry alligators, with their mouths open wide, stretched across it like a bridge.

Kwang-Su shut his eyes, to block out the sight before him. And there, in his mind, his master appeared.

"Be brave and be strong, boy," came the voice of Shun-Che, ringing in his head. "You can come through anything if you remember all that I have taught you."

With that, Kwang-Su felt his strength return. He went to open the box of little red seeds, but just as he was doing so, a fierce alligator reared up out of the river, pouncing on him. Kwang-Su screamed, for its huge teeth were about to sink deep into his leg.

Just in time, the boy took a firm hold of the wooden staff that his master had given him and forced it between the alligator's jaws, stopping them from shutting.

Then, rushing to the nearest tree, he climbed to the top and watched, terrified, as a hundred angry alligators crawled out of the river and made a circle around the tree.

And when he dared to take his eyes off them, Kwang-Su gasped, for there was his box, lying open on the riverbank, and the last three little red seeds lying on the ground beside it. He'd dropped it as he ran!

What if an alligator eats them? he thought. *What if the water they're splashing all around washes the seeds into the river?* He might be able to cross this one but, without any more seeds, he'd have no hope when it came to the last and most dangerous river.

The alligators waited, hissing and snarling, but slowly they grew still and crawled back, one by one, into the rushing waters.

And Kwang-Su was in luck, for as the last alligator slipped away, it trod on a seed, walking it back into the river.

As soon as the seed was wet, its magic took effect and the alligator found itself no bigger than a lizard, sitting at the bottom of a little stream. And all the other alligators did too.

"What clever little seeds!" cried Kwang-Su, climbing down from the tree to continue on his journey.

But suddenly he heard a terrible roar.

"Who dares to shrink our mighty rivers?"

Kwang-Su looked up to see a massive bare-chested Genie, striding over the hills towards him. He was ten times the boy's height, and his mighty chest and arms rippled as he moved.

The land shook as the Genie strode forward and then there he was, looming above the boy.

"Who do you think you are, coming here without asking us?" the Genie boomed, pointing an immense finger at him. **"Take that!"**

And, all in an instant, Kwang-Su's head was as cold as ice. He reached up, only to find that his hair was gone – every last strand of it!

"I mean you no harm, sir!" cried the boy. "Do not cast your spells on me!"

But the Genie only laughed at Kwang-Su's baldness and pointed at him again. Suddenly the young warrior was standing there without any clothes on!

"Give me back my clothes!" he yelled, and if he was cold before he was freezing now.

But the Genie was pointing at him again and shaking with laughter, and suddenly Kwang-Su fell to the ground, crying out in agony.

"Aah!" he cried, as a terrible pain cut through his lower back. "What have you done to me now?"

The Genie hadn't even laid a finger on him and yet it was worse, much worse, than any blow the boy's master had ever landed on him, when he was teaching him to fight.

"Stop your spells!" begged Kwang-Su, getting to his feet. "I promise you – I do not mean to leave your rivers like this for ever."

His teeth were chattering as he pulled out the box of little white seeds his mother had given him, for it was still there, deep in his pocket. "As soon as I've done what I've come to do, I'll throw one of these into each of your mighty rivers, and they'll be as big and strong as ever they were," he said.

"They'd better be," boomed the Genie, looking down at the seeds with a scowl, "or it'll be the end of you!"

He was impressed, though, at how brave the boy was in standing up to him. Impressed, too, at his strength in fighting off the power of his magic, for no human had ever before been able to return to his feet after a finger-blow to the back.

"Now what is it that brings you here, naked little human?" he giggled.

"I've come to find a jade pestle and mortar," replied the shivering boy, "for my future mother-in-law to mix her magic potions in."

"You've another river to cross, then." The Genie laughed. "But you'll never do it, for it's the Black River, a mile wide, and it's watched over by a terrible dragon."

"So how did you get across, if it's so difficult?" asked the boy.

"Oh, it's no bother to me," said the Genie. "I can fly, faster and higher than any dragon."

"Well, I can jump," said Kwang-Su, trying to sound brave. "But please, give me back my clothes and hair before I die of cold. And no more of your magic stabs in the back!"

"I will," said the Genie. "You're very brave for such a small, little human. And I'll come along with you on your journey, if you don't mind. It will be fun to watch you face the power and danger of our rivers – and even more fun to watch you fail!"

The boy touched the top of his head, and there was his pigtail, as before. He looked

down, and there were his clothes. He
wriggled his body, and the pain had gone
from his back.

So he picked up his box, put the last two
little red seeds back inside, and off he went.

Chapter 4
Dragon of the Deep

The Genie, who was only young as it turned out, went with him, and they set off together for the Black River.

But when they got there Kwang-Su's bravery was put to the test yet again, for what did he see but a great stretch of roaring water, as black as ink, reaching out in front of him for as far as the eye could see.

On a rock in the middle of the river, just as the Genie had said, sat a mighty dragon, breathing fire. And if the monsters Kwang-Su had come up against before had been frightening, this one would strike terror into even the bravest of souls.

"What shall I do?" muttered the young warrior, a cold shiver of fear running down his spine. "The seed will make the river shrink but I still won't be able to cross, for the dragon will remain, looking after its rock."

Just at that moment the monster lashed its mighty tail, which shot past the boy, missing his head by less than an inch. Kwang-Su gasped in horror, but when the dragon's tail returned to the rock, the boy noticed that the end of it was resting in the water.

"Be strong!" Kwang-Su told himself. "Be brave!" And he closed his eyes for a second

and saw Ling-Ling, there before him. "Be strong and brave for the girl you love!"

He pulled out the box of red seeds she'd given him, and tossed the fourth one into the rushing water.

In an instant the river dried up, leaving only a shallow stream running through the grass at their feet.

And when he looked to see what had become of the dragon, it seemed to have gone.

Only when he and the Genie got to the rock, in the middle of what had been the mighty river, did they see that there, still sitting on it, was a tiny dragonfly, glinting in the sun.

"That was lucky, boy!" cried the young Genie.

"Not lucky," replied Kwang-Su, with a shake of the head. "It was magic – the magic of the seeds."

The young Genie was puzzled. "Show me this magic you speak of, for I've seen nothing like it before."

Kwang-Su handed over the little box, which looked tiny in the hand of an enormous Genie.

"Where did this magic come from?" boomed the mighty one, opening the box and squinting at the seeds. "I thought only Genii had magic powers."

Kwang-Su told him, and the Genie nodded, thoughtfully.

"I will help you in your quest, boy," he vowed, "for even though you are only a feeble little human, I am very impressed by your magic, and how brave you are. But if you want a jade pestle and mortar, you will have to climb Mount Fumi with me," he said, pointing to the highest mountain, brushing the clouds with its peak. "Are you strong enough to get all the way to the top?"

"I am brave enough to try," said the boy.

Chapter 5
The Sea of Jewels

It was a long hard climb, through a day and a night, and there were many times when Kwang-Su thought he'd never make it. But the young Genie helped him when he needed it most and at last, together, they reached the top of the great mountain.

And there, by the light of the rising sun, Kwang-Su found eight Genii, each older and more powerful than the first. Each was sitting on his own snow-covered peak, looking down on the fabulous Sea of Jewels, which reached out below them on the other side.

Each had a long white beard, growing all the way down from his enormous grizzled head to his crooked feet. Each was bare-chested, despite the bitter cold, and each had muscles like snakes rippling through his massive body.

Kwang-Su stared at the beautiful sea below, flashing in the sun with every colour of the rainbow. He forgot all about the pestle and mortar he had come to collect, as he watched the waves rippling on the shore, washing up all kinds of gemstones – diamonds and rubies, sapphires and pearls.

Every single pebble was a precious stone, and the youth wanted very much to go down to the shores of the beautiful lake and fill his pockets with them.

The young Genie who had been his guide told the others why Kwang-Su had come, and all about the wonderful red and white seeds that he carried with him.

"This boy has special powers," he told them. "We must allow him to have the very last pestle and mortar or he will not give us our rivers back."

The eight older Genii knew that their younger friend was right, for it was the power of those four great rivers that stopped any human from ever reaching the Sea of Jewels and stealing away their treasures.

They were angry, though, for they didn't like the idea of a weak little human and a few tiny seeds having greater power than them.

"Let him have them, then ..." boomed one, with a voice that was like the rumble of thunder among the hills. "If he can carry them!"

And all eight of the mighty Genii held their massive bellies, as they laughed and laughed until the snow-clad peaks shook beneath them.

For it turned out that all of the human-sized pestle and mortars had already been used up, that the only mortar left was bigger than a man, and that the last remaining pestle was so heavy that no human could ever hope to lift it.

Chapter 6
The Last Red Sea

When Kwang-Su had finished gazing at the Sea of Jewels, he walked around the giant pestle and mortar, and wondered how on earth he could carry them back down the mountain and across the plains to Yun-Nan. He sat down beside them, to think the matter over, while the eight great Genii chuckled away.

"Take them if you can, boy," said one, teasing him. "And why not fill the mortar with precious stones while you're at it? For any man who can carry it empty, can carry it full."

Kwang-Su sat there, thinking. He hadn't studied for three years with the wisest master in the land for nothing, and besides, he was determined to marry Ling-Ling.

He closed his eyes then, and saw both of their faces, and that of his mother and father too. All four of them were smiling and encouraging him. Be brave! Be strong! Be wise!

Kwang-Su's ears had been closed to the Genii while he thought. But slowly, slowly, their words filtered through to his brain. "Fill the mortar with precious stones," one had said.

And suddenly Kwang-Su realised why he had been given five little red seeds, rather than four.

"Would you do me a favour?" he asked the younger Genie. "Would you make a heap of stones at the side of my mortar?"

"Why?" asked his friend.

"I want to look inside it, and I'm not tall enough to see over the rim."

"I will," replied the Genie, and he began to build some steps for the young man to climb.

Meanwhile, Kwang-Su ran down to the water and began stuffing his pockets with diamonds and rubies, emeralds and pearls.

When he'd gathered up as many as he could carry, he ran back up the mountain, climbed the steps the young Genie had made for him, and dropped the precious stones into the mortar.

Again and again he did this until it was quite full and held enough gems to make him

the richest man in China, richer even than the oldest, most powerful mandarin.

When Kwang-Su had filled the mortar so full that he couldn't fit in one more stone, he stood back and looked at the bowl of treasure.

"So what are you going to do with it now, boy?" asked one of the mighty Genii, watching him. "Take it on your head and carry it home?"

"No," replied the boy, with a smile. "I shall carry it under one arm." *For if I have the power to make rivers smaller,* he thought, *I must also have the power to shrink this bowl of jade.*

He took out his little box, dropped the last red seed on top of the precious stones, and it happened, just as he'd hoped – the pestle and mortar shrank, all in an instant, to normal size!

Kwang-Su picked up the pestle and slipped it into his pocket. Then he lifted the mortar as carefully as he could, so as not to spill the precious stones.

"Goodbye," he said, bowing to the surprised Genii, "and thank you for allowing me to take home so many of your riches." And off he went.

Behind him he heard a mighty roar, as if a hundred and fifty lions were waiting to be fed.

The Genii were very angry at being tricked, and at losing so much of their treasure. But they knew better than to stop Kwang-Su, for only he had the power to turn their four tiny streams back into mighty rivers.

Chapter 7
Ling-Ling

On his way back the boy did exactly as he had promised. He jumped across the first brook, threw one of the white seeds his mother had given him into the water and instantly it turned back into a terrible inky black river, a mile wide, with a mighty fire-breathing dragon on a rock in the middle.

And the roars of the Genii went quiet when they saw the Black River rolling once more between them and the outside world.

At the Red River, the alligators wanted to get their revenge on Kwang-Su. But the boy, once he had returned the water to its natural state, was just about able to keep clear of their snapping jaws.

At the White River and the Blue River, Kwang-Su did the same.

And from that day to this no one else has ever been to the home of the Genii, because not a single person can cross even one of the powerful rivers.

For seven more days the boy walked on, and he came at last to his parents' home in Yo-Chan. They were delighted to see their only son, safe and well!

And when he gave his mother a precious stone for every seed she'd given him – a diamond, a ruby, an emerald, and a sapphire, each as large as an egg, they were over the moon.

He went on then to Yun-nan, to find Ling-Ling.

"Go away, boy," hissed the girl's mother, when she opened the door and saw who it was. "You're too late!"

"What do you mean, too late?" cried Kwang-Su. "I have crossed four mighty rivers, climbed the highest mountains, faced eight angry Genii, and fetched you back the jade pestle and mortar you asked for – the very last one in the world! And not only that, old woman," he said, pulling out piles of precious stones from his pockets, "but I have brought you these! Look, I am now richer than the rich old mandarin. How dare you say I am not fit to marry your daughter?"

"Oh, dear," said the woman, all confused. "I never thought you stood a chance! But, Kwang-Su ..." and she dropped her voice to a whisper. "You must leave, now, for all my friends are here, in the garden. They have come for Ling-Ling's marriage to the old mandarin."

"Today?" the boy gasped.

"Yes, today," the woman told him.

"And are they married yet?"

The woman was silent, then.

"Tell me!" hissed Kwang-Su. "You must tell me!"

"No, not yet," the woman admitted. "The wedding is just beginning."

Kwang-Su pushed past her and raced out into the garden.

"**Stop!**" he yelled.

People turned to look, and Ling-Ling almost fainted when she saw who it was. "Kwang-Su!" she cried. "My mother told me you were dead!" And she rushed towards him, throwing herself into his arms.

But Ling-Ling's mother was at the boy's side. "Go away before everyone sees you!" she hissed. "The old mandarin will be furious with me, and all my guests will think I am a fool! Leave quickly, Kwang-Su, and I will buy the jade pestle and mortar from you with some of the money he has given me."

"No!" yelled Kwang-Su, who suddenly knew what to do. He pulled out the very last little white seed, dropped it into the mortar, which grew in size instantly, until it filled the plot of grass beneath the peach tree and was full of glittering jewels.

Then Kwang-Su climbed up into the tree, plucking rubies and diamonds and all kinds of precious stones from the giant mortar and throwing them down, all among the wedding guests.

Some stood and stared, but a few ran about, grabbing as many as they could. And the most frantic of all was the monkey-faced mandarin, who turned his back on Ling-Ling, pushed people out of the way, and scrabbled around on the grass to find every last jewel.

"How greedy he is!" said the others, watching. "You wouldn't think, to look at him, that he was already one of the richest men in the land, and that even his teacups are set with diamonds!"

Kwang-Su went up to the greedy old mandarin and offered him his three largest rubies, each the size of a hen's egg, if he would go away and say nothing about marrying Ling-Ling ever again.

And the old mandarin, who cared much more for riches than for love, agreed.

Kwang-Su and Ling-Ling were married soon after, in the city where his mother and father lived.

Most of the treasures Kwang-Su had brought back from the Sea of Jewels were given to the poor of the city, and he and his young wife were as happy as they should be.

BATTLE CARDS

Malachy Doyle

Author

Favourite hero:
Young Lambton (in *The Lambton Curse*).
Favourite monster:
The Worm (in *The Lambton Curse*).
Your weapon of choice:
A lollipop.
Special secret power:
I can turn Man-Eating Monsters into
little mice with my Amazing Lollipop.
Favourite fight scene:
The one where I meet Haranga the
Horrible, he grabs my lollipop, licks it,
and turns into a tiny squeaker.
Goodie or Baddie:
A goodie pretending to be a baddie
pretending to be a goodie.

RELOADED

Nana Li

Illustrator

Favourite hero:
The Monkey King in *The Journey to the West*.

Favourite monster:
The Ghost of Canterville ... if that counts as a monster.

Your weapon of choice:
The Monkey King's magic stick.

Special secret power:
Shape shifting.

Goodie or Baddie:
Whether you see me as good or bad probably depends on whether you're my friend or my foe, but I do find it hard to be evil.

RELOADED

Barrington Stoke would like to thank all its readers for commenting on the manuscript before publication and in particular:

Sam Blower
Leon Bryson
Jaime-Louise Dewis
Ryan King
Sam Lavender
Sean O'Neill
Jack Ramsay
Danielle Rear
Megan Reynolds
Kate Rooney
Katie Rutler
Nilani Sivanantharajah
Steven
Alex Taylor

Become a Consultant!

Would you like to be a consultant? Ask your parent, carer or teacher to contact us at the email address below – we'd love to hear from them! They can also find out more by visiting our website.

schools@barringtonstoke.co.uk
www.barringtonstoke.co.uk